The Wizard
of Oz

FAMILY LEARNING

from Dorling Kindersley

The Family Learning mission is to support the concept of the home as a center of learning and to help families develop independent learning skills to last a lifetime.

Editor Rebecca Smith
Senior Art Editor Jane Thomas
Senior Editor Marie Greenwood
Managing Art Editor Jacquie Gulliver
Picture Research Cynthia Frazer
US Editor Constance Robinson
DTP Designer Kim Browne
Production Joanne Rooke

Published by Family Learning
Southland Executive Park, 7800 Southland Boulevard
Orlando, Florida 32809

Dorling Kindersley registered offices:
9 Henrietta Street, Covent Garden, London WC2E 8PS

www.dk.com

Color reproduction by Bright Arts, Hong Kong
Printed in Italy by L.E.G.O.

Morris, Kimberly.
The Wizard of Oz / by L. Frank Baum ; adapted by Kimberly Morris ;
illustrated by Mauro Evangelista. -- 1st American ed.
p.   cm. -- (Young Classics)
Summary: A simplified retelling of Dorothy's adventures after a
cyclone transports her to the land of Oz and she must seek out the
great wizard in order to return to Kansas.
ISBN 0-7894-4444-5
[1. Fantasy.] I. Baum, L. Frank (Lyman Frank), 1856–1919.
Wizard of Oz. II. Evangelista, Mauro, ill. III Title.
IV. Series.
PZ7. M82833Wi   1999
[Fic]--dc21   98-45494
                                                                              CIP
                                                                              AP

Acknowledgements
The publisher would like to thank the following for their kind permission to reproduce their photographs:

a = above; c = center; b = below; l = left; r = right; t = top.
Jean-Loup Charmet: 17 tr; **Corbis UK Ltd:** 46 cl, 48 cra; © **Crown Copyright: Historic Royal Palaces:**14 bl; **Del Rey Books**, published by Ballantine Books, New York /Cover art by Michael Herring: 48 br; **Dover Publications Inc** © **1986:** 46 tl, 48 clb; **Mary Evans Picture Library:** 20 bc; **Ronald Grant Archive /MGM:** 46 br, 47 cra, 47 bl, back jacket cr; **Image Bank** Steve Bronstein 7 tr; **Kansas State Historical Society:** 44 bl; **Kobal Collection/MGM:** 46 cr, 47 tr, 47 tl; **Vintage Magazine Co. Ltd:** 47crb, 48tl, inside back flap.

The publisher would particularly like to thank the following people:
Andy Crawford and Gary Ombler (photography); Chris Molan and Sallie Alane Reason
(additional illustration); Claire Jones (models); Claire Ricketts (design assistance).

YOUNG CLASSICS

The Wizard of Oz

By L. FRANK BAUM
Adapted by Kimberly Morris

Illustrated by
Mauro Evangelista

FAMILY LEARNING

Illustration by W.W. Denslow from
The Wonderful Wizard of Oz, *1900*

Contents

The Cyclone

Dorothy lived on the Kansas prairie with Uncle Henry, a farmer, and Aunt Em. Their house was small, and there was no cellar except a small hole dug in the ground where the family could go in case one of those great whirlwinds arose.

When Dorothy stood in the doorway, she could see nothing but the great gray prairie on every side. Not a tree nor a house broke the broad sweep of flat country.

When Aunt Em came to live there, she was a young, pretty wife. But the sun and wind had taken the sparkle from her eyes and left them a sober gray. When Dorothy, who was an orphan, first came, Aunt Em had been startled by the child's laughter. Uncle Henry never laughed. He was gray also, from his long beard to his rough boots.

It was Toto that made Dorothy laugh, and

"There's a cyclone coming!"

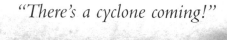

saved her from growing gray. Toto was a little black dog with eyes that twinkled merrily. Dorothy loved him dearly, and they played together all day long.

The cyclone in the story is really a tornado. These great spiraling winds can lift whole houses up into the air!

Today, however, they were not playing. Uncle Henry looked anxiously at the sky, which was grayer than usual. From the far north, he heard a low wailing wind.

"There's a cyclone coming! I'll go look after the stock." He ran towards the cows and horses.

Aunt Em dropped her work. "Quick, Dorothy," she screamed, "run for the cellar!" Aunt Em threw open the trapdoor in the floor and climbed down into the dark hole. Dorothy caught Toto and started to follow. She was halfway across the room when there came a great shriek from the wind. The house shook so hard that she lost her footing. Then, a strange thing happened. The house whirled around three times and rose slowly through the air.

The wind raised it higher and higher, until it was at the very top of the cyclone. Hour after hour passed, until at last Dorothy crawled over the floor to her bed. Toto lay down beside her. In spite of the swaying of the house and the wailing of the wind, Dorothy closed her eyes and fell fast asleep.

Dorothy was awakened by a shock, sudden and severe as the house landed. She sprang from her bed with Toto at her heels and gave a cry of amazement. The cyclone had set the house down in a country of marvelous beauty. There were stately trees, banks of flowers, and birds with brilliant plumage.

While she stood looking, she noticed a group of the oddest people. They were not as big as the grown folk she had been used to. Three were men all dressed in blue, and one a woman in a white gown. The little woman walked up to Dorothy, made a low bow, and said in a sweet voice, "Welcome to the land of the Munchkins. We are grateful to you for having killed the Wicked Witch of the East, and for setting our people free."

"Welcome to the land of the Munchkins."

Dorothy listened with wonder. "There must be some mistake," she said. "I have not killed anything."

"Your house did," replied the woman. "See!"

Just under the corner of the house, two feet were sticking out, shod in silver shoes.

"Oh, dear!" cried Dorothy in dismay. "What ever shall we do?"

"There is nothing to be done," said the little woman. "The Wicked Witch of the East held all the Munchkins in bondage. Now they are free."

"Are you a Munchkin?" asked Dorothy.

"No, I am the Witch of the North. But I am a good witch. There were four witches in the Land of Oz. Those who live in the North and the South are good. Those who dwell in the East and the West are wicked. Now that you have killed one of them, there is but one wicked Witch left – the one who lives in the West."

Just then, the Munchkins gave a loud shout and pointed to the house. The woman looked and began to laugh. The feet of the dead Witch had disappeared entirely and nothing was left but the silver shoes. "She was so old that she dried up quickly in the sun. But the silver shoes are yours, and you shall have them to wear." She handed them to Dorothy.

"There is some charm connected with them, but what it is we never knew," said one of the Munchkins.

"I am anxious to get back to my Aunt and Uncle. Can you help me find my way?" asked Dorothy.

The woman took off her cap and balanced the point on the end of her nose. At once, the cap changed to a slate, on which was written in white chalk marks:

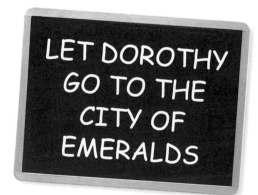

LET DOROTHY
GO TO THE
CITY OF
EMERALDS

The Yellow Brick Road

THE WOMAN TOOK the slate from her nose. "You must go to the City of Emeralds. It is in the center of the country, and is ruled by Oz, the great Wizard. I will give you my kiss as protection." She came close to Dorothy and kissed her gently on the forehead, leaving a shining mark. "The road to the City of Emeralds is paved with yellow brick, so you cannot miss it. When you get to Oz, tell your story to the Wizard and ask him to help you. Good-bye, my dear."

Farmers put scarecrows in fields to scare crows and other birds away from the crops.

"Come along, Toto," said Dorothy, "we will go to the Emerald City and ask the great Oz how to get back to Kansas."

So Dorothy started along the road of yellow brick. After a while she came to a fence, beyond which was a great cornfield – and in it was a Scarecrow on a pole.

Dorothy gazed at the painted face of the Scarecrow. Suddenly, to her great surprise, one of the eyes winked at her. Then the figure nodded its head in a friendly way.

Dorothy walked up to it.

"Can't you get down?" she asked.

"No, for this pole is stuck up my back," replied the Scarecrow.

Dorothy reached up and lifted the figure off the pole.

Being stuffed with straw, it was quite light. "Thank you very much," said the Scarecrow. "I feel like a new man."

Dorothy was puzzled at this, for it sounded odd to hear a stuffed man speak.

"Who are you?" asked the Scarecrow when he had stretched himself.

"My name is Dorothy," said the girl. "I am going to the Emerald City to ask the great Oz to send me back to Kansas."

"Do you think," he asked,

Dorothy walked up to the Scarecrow.

"that Oz would give me some brains? I do not want people to call me a fool. And if my head stays stuffed with straw instead of with brains, how am I ever to know anything?"

"I cannot tell, but if you come with me, I'll ask Oz to do all he can for you."

"Thank you," he answered, gratefully.

So they started along the path of yellow brick.

"Tell me about yourself, and the country you came from," said the Scarecrow.

She told him about Kansas, and how gray everything was there. The Scarecrow looked puzzled, "I cannot understand why you want to leave this beautiful country and go back to such a gray place."

Dorothy explained, "No matter how dreary and gray our homes are, we people of flesh and blood would rather live there than in any other country. There is no place like home."

After an hour or so the light faded away, and they found themselves stumbling along in darkness.

The Scarecrow stopped. "I see a cottage. Shall we go there?"

"Yes, indeed," answered the child. "I am all tired out."

Inside the cottage, Dorothy found a bed of leaves gathered in one corner. She lay down and, with Toto beside her, fell into a sound sleep. But the Scarecrow, who was never tired, stood and waited patiently.

When Dorothy awoke, the sun was shining. The two travelers left the cottage and walked through the trees until they heard a deep groan. Startled, Dorothy stopped and looked around.

One of the big trees had been partly chopped through. Standing beside it, with an uplifted axe, was a man made entirely of tin. He stood perfectly motionless. Dorothy looked at him in amazement.

"Please get an oilcan," the Tin Woodman requested. "My joints are rusted so badly I cannot move. You will find an oilcan on a shelf in my cottage."

There was a man made entirely of tin.

Dorothy ran back to the cottage and returned with the oilcan. "Oil my neck, first," said the Tin Woodman.

Dorothy oiled it, and the Scarecrow took hold of the tin head and moved it gently until the man could turn it himself.

"Now oil the joints in my arms," he said.

The Tin Woodman is very polite and grateful to Dorothy for oiling his joints, but he still thinks he needs a heart!

Dorothy oiled them and the Tin Woodman gave a sigh of relief, lowering his axe. "This is a great comfort."

When they had oiled his legs until he could move them freely, he thanked them again and again for he was a very polite creature. "I might have stood there forever if you had not come along," he said. "How did you happen to be here?"

"We are on our way to see the great Oz," she answered. "I want him to send me back to Kansas, and the Scarecrow wants him to put brains into his head."

The Tin Woodman appeared to think deeply. "If you will allow me to join your party, I will ask Oz to give me a heart."

"Come along," the Scarecrow said heartily, and Dorothy added that she would be pleased to have his company.

And so Dorothy, the Scarecrow, and the Tin Woodman set off through the thick woods. The road was still paved with yellow bricks, but these were covered by dried branches and dead leaves from the trees. Now and then there came a deep growl from some animal hidden among the trees. These sounds made the little girl's heart beat fast, for she did not know what made them.

"How long will it be," the child asked the Tin Woodman, "before we are out of the forest?"

"I cannot tell," was the answer.

Just as he spoke, there came from the forest a terrible roar, and the next moment a great Lion bounded into the road.

Little Toto ran barking toward the Lion, and the great beast opened his mouth.

Dorothy, fearing Toto would be killed, rushed forward and slapped the Lion upon his nose, while she cried out, "Don't you dare to bite Toto! You ought to be ashamed of yourself, a big beast like you, to bite a poor little dog."

"I didn't bite him," said the Lion, as he rubbed his nose with his paw.

"No, but you tried to," she retorted. "You are nothing but a big coward."

"I know it," said the Lion, hanging his head in shame. "I learned that if I roared loudly every living thing was frightened and got out of my way. But if the elephants and tigers had ever tried to fight me, I should have run myself – I'm such a coward."

"The King of Beasts shouldn't be a coward," said the Scarecrow.

"I know it," returned the Lion, wiping a tear from his eye with the tip of his tail. "It makes my life very unhappy. Whenever there is danger my heart begins to beat fast."

"You ought to be glad," said the Tin Woodman, "for it proves you have a heart. I have no heart."

"Perhaps," said the Lion thoughtfully, "if I had no heart I should not be a coward."

"Have you brains?" asked the Scarecrow.

"I suppose so. I've never looked to see," replied the Lion.

"I am going to the great Oz to ask him to give me some," remarked the Scarecrow.

"And I am going to ask him to give me a heart," said the Woodman.

"And I am going to ask him to send Toto and me back to Kansas,"

Because of its legendary strength and courage, the lion is often thought of as king of the beasts. However, this lion is a scaredy-cat!

"I didn't bite him,"
said the Lion.

added Dorothy.

"Do you think Oz could
give me courage?" asked the Lion.

"Just as easily as he could give me brains," said the Scarecrow.

"Or give me a heart," said the Tin Woodman.

"Or send me back to Kansas," said Dorothy.

"Then I'll go with you," said the Lion, "for my life is simply
unbearable without a bit of courage."

The Journey to Oz

"YOU WILL BE VERY WELCOME," answered Dorothy, "for you will help to keep away the other wild beasts. It seems to me they must be more cowardly than you are if they allow you to scare them so easily."

"They are," said the Lion, "but that doesn't make me any braver."

So once more the little company set off upon the journey, the Lion walking with stately strides at Dorothy's side, until they came to a forest. The Lion whispered that this was where the Kalidahs lived.

"What are the Kalidahs?" asked Dorothy.

"They are beasts with bodies like bears and heads like tigers," replied the Lion, "and with claws so long they could tear me in two. I'm terribly afraid of the Kalidahs."

After a while, they came to a gulf across the road, broad and deep.

"Here is a tree," the Scarecrow said. "If the Tin Woodman can chop it down, so that it falls to the other side, we can walk across it."

"That is a first-rate idea," said the Lion. "One would almost suspect you had brains."

The Woodman set to work and the big tree fell across the ditch. They had just started to cross when, to their horror, they saw two great beasts behind them.

"Kalidahs!" said the Cowardly Lion, trembling.

"Quick," cried the Scarecrow, "let us cross over."

Dorothy went first, holding Toto. The Tin Woodman followed, and the Scarecrow came next. The Lion, although he was afraid, turned to face the Kalidahs and gave a terrible roar. The fierce beasts stopped and looked at him in surprise. But, seeing they were bigger than the Lion, the Kalidahs rushed forward. The Lion crossed over the tree and turned to see what they would do next. The fierce beasts also began to cross the tree.

The Lion said to Dorothy, "We are lost, for they will surely tear us to pieces. But I will fight them as long as I am alive."

"Wait," called the Scarecrow, and he asked the Woodman to chop away the end of the tree that rested on their side of the ditch. The Tin Woodman began to use his axe, and, just as the Kalidahs were nearly across, the tree fell with a crash into the gulf, carrying the ugly, snarling brutes with it.

This adventure made the travelers anxious to get out of the forest, and they walked so fast that Dorothy became tired and had to ride on the Lion's back.

There are many mythical creatures that are made up of two types of animals. One of the best known is the griffin (above), which is part lion, part eagle.

The Lion gave a terrible roar.

To their great joy, the trees became
thinner as they walked onward, and
in the afternoon, they came upon a
broad river. "How shall we cross it?"
asked Dorothy.

*The Stork carried
the Scarecrow to
the bank.*

"The Tin Woodman must build us
a raft," replied the Scarecrow.

After the Tin Woodman had cut logs
and fastened them together with wooden
pins, they were ready to start.

The Scarecrow and the Tin Woodman had long poles to
push the raft through the water. They got along quite well at first. But
when they reached the middle of the river, the Scarecrow pushed so
hard on his pole that it stuck fast in the mud at the bottom. Before he
could pull it out, the raft was swept away and the poor Scarecrow was
left clinging to the pole in the middle of the river.

When they reached the shore, they sat down and gazed wistfully
at the Scarecrow until a Stork flew by. The big bird flew into the air
and over the water till she came to where the Scarecrow was perched
upon his pole. Then the Stork grabbed the Scarecrow by the arm
and carried him to the bank.

When the Scarecrow found himself among his friends again, he
was so happy he hugged them all.

"Thank you," said Dorothy to the kind Stork before it flew out
of sight.

They walked along listening to
the singing of the birds and looking
at the lovely flowers. The ground
was carpeted with scarlet poppies,
which were so brilliant in color they
almost dazzled Dorothy's eyes.

"Aren't they beautiful?" said

*Poppies have been
associated with sleep
and death since
storytelling began. Poppy
seeds contain opium, a
drug that causes sleepiness.*

Dorothy, as she breathed in the scent of the flowers.

Now it is well known that when there are many of these flowers together their odor is so powerful that anyone who breathes it falls asleep. If the sleeper is not carried away from the scent, he sleeps on forever. But Dorothy did not know this, and her eyes grew heavy.

"We must hurry," the Tin Woodman said.

They kept walking until Dorothy could stand no longer and she fell among the poppies, fast asleep.

"If we leave her she will die," said the Lion. "The smell of the flowers is killing us all."

It was true, Toto had fallen down beside his little mistress. But the Scarecrow and the Tin Woodman, not being made of flesh, were not troubled by the scent.

"Run fast," said the Scarecrow to the Lion. "Get out of this deadly flowerbed as soon as you can. We will bring Dorothy, but if you should fall asleep, you are too big to be carried."

The Lion shook himself and bounded forward as fast as he could go.

The Lion bounded forward.

"Let us make a chair with our hands and carry her," said the Scarecrow. So they put Toto in Dorothy's lap and carried the sleeping girl through the flowers.

They pulled the Lion out of the poppy bed.

At last, they came upon the Lion, fast asleep among the poppies. The flowers had been too strong for the huge beast.

"He is too heavy to lift," the Tin Woodman said sadly. "We must leave him here to sleep on forever."

They carried Dorothy to a place far from the poppy field and waited for the fresh breeze to waken her.

Suddenly, the Tin Woodman saw a strange beast come bounding toward them. It was a great wildcat. As it came nearer, the Tin Woodman saw that it was chasing a little field mouse. Although he had no heart he knew it was wrong for the wildcat to try to kill such a harmless creature.

The Woodman raised his axe. As the wildcat ran by, he gave it a quick blow and cut off the beast's head.

The field mouse stopped and said, "Oh, thank you! Thank you for saving my life. I am the Queen of the field mice."

In a fable by Aesop, a mouse saves a lion by nibbling through the net the lion is caught in. In The Wizard of Oz, *Baum shows how small, seemingly weak creatures have strength in numbers.*

At that moment, several mice ran up. One of the biggest mice spoke. "Is there anything we can do to repay you for saving the life of our Queen?"

"Yes," the Scarecrow said quickly, "you can save our friend, the Cowardly Lion, who is asleep in the poppy bed."

The Queen turned to the mice and told them to gather all her people together. The Scarecrow told the Woodman to make a truck from the trees by the riverside. When the truck was ready, the mice came from all directions, and each one brought a piece of string. As Dorothy woke from her long sleep, she was

greatly astonished to see thousands of mice looking at her timidly. The truck was a thousand times bigger than any of the mice, but once they had been harnessed they were able to pull it quite easily. The Scarecrow and Tin Woodman sat on it, and were drawn swiftly to where the Lion lay asleep.

They lifted the Lion onto the truck and the little creatures pulled the Lion out of the poppy bed to the green fields, where he could breath fresh air again. Once unharnessed from the truck, the mice scampered away.

"If ever you need us again," the Queen of the Mice said, "come out into the field and call. We shall hear and come to your assistance. Good-bye!" And away the Queen ran.

The Emerald City

S O, WHEN THE LION was fully refreshed, they started again upon the journey, enjoying the walk through the soft, fresh grass. Soon they saw a green glow in the sky. "That must be the Emerald City," said Dorothy.

Emeralds are beautiful green gems. The sparkling greenness of Emerald City makes it seem enchanting and wonderful.

At last they came to a great wall studded with emeralds. There was a bell beside the gate. Dorothy pushed the button. The big gate swung slowly open, and they found themselves in a high arched room. The walls glistened with emeralds.

Before them stood a little man clothed all in green. "What do you wish in the Emerald City?" he asked.

"We came here to see the Great Oz," said Dorothy.

"I am the Guardian of the Gates, and since you demand to see the Great Oz I must take you to his palace. But first you must put on spectacles. If you do not wear spectacles, the brightness of the Emerald City will blind you."

He opened a big box full of spectacles. All of them had green glasses in them. The Guardian of the Gates found a pair that would fit Dorothy. Then he found spectacles for the Scarecrow and the Tin Woodman and the Lion, and even little Toto.

The Guardian of the Gates put on his own glasses. Taking a big golden key from a peg on the wall, he opened another gate, and they followed him through the portal into the streets of the Emerald City.

Even with their eyes protected by spectacles, Dorothy and her friends were dazzled by the wonderful City. The streets were lined with beautiful houses, all built of green marble. The windowpanes were of green glass, and even the sky above the City had a green tint.

The Guardian of the Gates led them through the streets until they came to the Palace of Oz.

There was a soldier before the door.

"Here are strangers," said the Guardian of the Gates. "They demand to see the Great Oz."

"I will carry your message to him," answered the soldier.

They had to wait a long time before the soldier returned. "He will grant you an audience, but each one of you must enter his presence alone, and he will admit only one each day. I will have you shown to rooms where you may rest."

The Guardian took a big golden key from a peg on the wall.

The next morning, Dorothy was taken into a round room with a high roof. A huge throne of green marble stood in the middle. In the center of the throne was an enormous Head without a body. As Dorothy gazed at the head, it started to speak. "I am Oz, the Great and Terrible," said the Head. "Where did you get the silver shoes?"

"From the Wicked Witch of the East. My house fell on her and killed her," Dorothy replied.

"And where did you get the mark upon your forehead?" the voice continued.

"That is where the Good Witch of the North kissed me," said Dorothy.

"What do you wish me to do?" boomed the voice.

"Send me back to Kansas," she answered.

"Well," said the Head. "You have no right to expect me to send you back to Kansas unless you do something for me in return."

"I am Oz the Great and Terrible."

"What must I do?"

"Kill the Wicked Witch of the West."

Dorothy began to weep. "Even if I wanted to, how could I kill the Wicked Witch?"

"I do not know," said the Head, "but that is my answer. Now go."

The next morning, the Scarecrow was admitted into the Throne Room, where he saw a lovely lady. She looked upon him sweetly and said, "I am Oz, the Great and Terrible. Why do you seek me?"

"I come to you praying that you

The Scarecrow saw a lovely lady.

will put brains in my head."

"If you will kill the Wicked Witch of the West I will bestow upon you such good brains that you will be the wisest man in all the Land of Oz. Now go."

The next morning the Tin Woodman came to the great Throne Room. But when he entered, Oz had taken the shape of a terrible beast. "Why do you seek me?"

"I ask you to give me a heart."

"Help Dorothy to kill the Wicked Witch of the West," replied the Beast, "and I will give you the biggest and kindest heart in all the Land of Oz."

The next morning the Lion passed through the door and saw a Ball of Fire.

"I ask you to give me a heart," said the Tin Woodman.

A low, quiet voice came from the Fire. "Why do you seek me?"

"I come to you to beg that you give me courage," said the Lion.

"Bring me proof that the Wicked Witch is dead, and I will give you courage," the fire replied.

The Lion turned tail and rushed from the room. He was glad to see his friends waiting for him. They talked about what they had heard.

"What shall we do?" asked Dorothy, sadly.

"There is only one thing we can do," returned the Lion, "and that is to seek out the Wicked Witch, and destroy her."

"Bring me proof that the Wicked Witch is dead," said the voice.

The Wicked Witch of the West

In many legends, magic caps give the wearer invisibility. But this golden cap gives the wearer control over the winged monkeys.

THE FRIENDS SET OFF toward the West. Now the Wicked Witch of the West had but one eye, but it was as powerful as a telescope. As she sat in the door of her castle, she saw Dorothy with her friends. Angry to find them in her country, the Wicked Witch blew upon a silver whistle. A pack of wolves came running.

"Tear them to pieces," said the Wicked Witch.

The Tin Woodman heard the wolves coming. He seized his axe and chopped them up until they all lay dead.

The Wicked Witch called her slaves, the Winkies, and gave them sharp spears. The Winkies were not brave people, but they had to do as they were told. They marched until they came near Dorothy. But the Lion sprang toward them, and the poor Winkies ran away as fast as they could.

The Wicked Witch sat down to think.

There was, in her cupboard, a Golden Cap encircled with jewels. Whoever owned it could call three times upon the Winged Monkeys, who obeyed any order. Twice already the Witch had used the Cap.

But there was only one way to destroy Dorothy and her friends. She took the Golden Cap, stood on her left foot, and said slowly,
"Ep-pe, pe-pe, kak-ke!"

The charm began to work.

The sky darkened. There was a rushing of many wings, and the Winged Monkeys flew to Dorothy and her friends.

There was a rushing of many wings.

Some of the Monkeys seized the Tin Woodman and carried him through the air. They dropped the poor Woodman, who fell a great distance. He lay so battered that he could neither move nor groan. Others caught the Scarecrow and pulled all the straw out of his clothes and head.

The remaining Monkeys threw a strong rope around the Lion. They flew with him to the Witch's castle, where he was placed in a yard with a high iron fence.

The King of the Winged Monkeys flew up to Dorothy. He saw the Good Witch's kiss upon her forehead. "We dare not harm this little girl," he said. "She is protected by the Power of Good. All we can do is carry her to the Wicked Witch's castle and leave her."

Carefully and gently they lifted Dorothy and carried her through the air to the castle. Then the King said to the Witch, "We have obeyed you but now your power over our band is ended."

Then all the Winged Monkeys flew out of sight.

The Wicked Witch noticed the mark on
Dorothy's forehead, then she looked down at Dorothy's
feet and saw the Silver Shoes. She laughed to herself and
thought, "I can make her my slave, for she does not know
how to use her power."

The Witch set Dorothy to work – cleaning pots and
kettles and sweeping the floor. Sometimes the Witch
threatened to beat her, though in truth she did not dare
strike Dorothy, because of the mark upon her forehead.
But the child did not know this, and was full of
fear. Dorothy's life became very sad.
Sometimes she would cry for hours, with
Toto sitting at her feet.

Now the Witch had a great longing to
own the silver shoes. But the child was so
proud of her pretty shoes that she never
took them off except when she took a
bath.

The Witch's dread of water was
great so she never came near when
Dorothy was bathing, but soon she
thought of a trick. She placed an
iron bar in the middle of the
kitchen floor and made the
bar invisible.

Dorothy was working in
the kitchen when she
walked across the floor and
stumbled over the bar. One
of the silver shoes came off!
Before Dorothy could reach
it, the Witch had put it on

her own foot. Dorothy was very shocked and cried out, "You have no right to take my shoe!"

"I shall keep it, just the same," said the Witch, laughing, "and some day I shall get the other one from you, too."

This made Dorothy so angry, she picked up a bucket of water and dashed it over the Witch. The wicked woman gave a loud cry.

"See what you have done!" she screamed. "In a minute I shall melt away."

"I'm very sorry, indeed," said Dorothy, who was truly frightened to see the Witch melting away like brown sugar.

"Look out – here I go!"

According to legend, witches are frightened of water. Baum takes this idea one step further – his Wicked Witch is melted by water!

With these words, the Witch fell down in a brown, melted mass and began to spread over the kitchen floor.

After picking out the silver shoe, which was all that was left of the old woman, Dorothy ran out to the courtyard to tell the Lion that the Wicked Witch of the West had come to an end. Dorothy then called all the Winkies together and told them they were no longer slaves.

There was great rejoicing among the yellow Winkies, for the Wicked Witch had always treated them with great cruelty. They kept this day as a holiday, then and ever after.

Dorothy picked up a bucket of water and dashed it over the Witch.

A number of the Winkies traveled to where the Tin Woodman lay. They carried him back to the castle and set to work until at last he was straightened out into his old form.

He wept tears of joy. "If only we had the Scarecrow with us, I should be quite happy."

"We must try to find him," said Dorothy. She called the Winkies and they walked until they came to the Scarecrow's clothes.

Dorothy asked the Winkies to carry them back to the castle, where they were stuffed with clean straw. At last! Here was the Scarecrow as good as ever.

"We must go back to Oz, and claim our rewards," said Dorothy.

The Winkies had grown so fond of the Tin Woodman that they begged him to stay and rule over them. But finding he was determined to go, they gave him a silver oilcan set with jewels.

Dorothy went to the Witch's cupboard and saw the Golden Cap. She did not know about the charm of the Cap, but she saw that it was pretty and made up her mind to wear it. Then, the four friends started for the Emerald City.

Days passed and they saw nothing but fields. "We have lost our way," the Scarecrow said.

"Suppose we call the Field Mice," Dorothy suggested. "They could probably tell us the way."

In a few minutes, many small gray mice came running. Among them was the Queen.

The Winkies set to work on the Tin Woodman.

"What can I do for my friends?"

"Can you tell us where the Emerald City is?" asked Dorothy.

"It is a great way off," replied the Queen, but then she noticed Dorothy's Golden Cap. "Why don't you use the charm of the Golden Cap and call the Winged Monkeys?"

"I didn't know there was a charm," said Dorothy.

"It is written in the Cap."

"Won't they hurt me?" asked the girl.

"No. They must obey the wearer of the Cap."

Dorothy looked inside the Golden Cap and read the directions. **"Ep-pe, pep-pe, kak-ke!"** she said, standing on her left foot.

The Scarecrow's clothes were stuffed with clean straw.

They soon heard a great chattering and flapping of wings as the Winged Monkeys flew up to them. The King bowed. "What is your command?"

"We wish to go the Emerald City," said the child.

"We will carry you," replied the King.

So they rode through the air quite cheerfully, until the strange creatures set the travelers down before the gates of the Emerald City.

The next morning the friends went into the Throne Room of the Great Oz – and saw no one. A voice, seeming to come from near the dome, said, "I am Oz, the Great and Terrible. Why do you seek me?"

"We have come to claim our promise," Dorothy said.

"Is the Wicked Witch destroyed?" asked the Voice.

"Yes," she answered. "I melted her."

"Dear me," said the Voice. "I must have time to think it over."

"But you must keep your promises!" Dorothy exclaimed.

Suddenly, the Lion gave a loud roar. Toto jumped and tipped over the screen in a corner. It fell, and all of them saw a little old man who seemed to be as surprised as they were.

The Tin Woodman raised his axe. "Who are you?"

"I am Oz," said the little man. "Don't strike me."

"Are you not a great Wizard?" cried Dorothy.

"I'm supposed to be a Wizard, but I'm just a common man. If you step this way, I will show you my tricks."

In one corner of the room lay a Great Head made out of paper. "I hung this from the ceiling," he said to Dorothy. Then he showed the Scarecrow the dress and mask he had worn when he seemed to be a Lady. The Tin Woodman saw that his Terrible Beast was nothing but a lot of skins sewn together. As for the Ball of Fire – it was really a ball of cotton, which burned fiercely when oil was poured onto it.

"You ought to be ashamed of yourself," said the Scarecrow.

"I am," said the man, "but let me tell you my story. I was born in Omaha. When I grew up, I became a balloonist. One day I went up and I couldn't come down. I traveled through the air. By the second day, I found myself in the midst of a strange people who thought I was a Wizard. Of course, I let them think so. I ordered them to build this Emerald City, and I put green spectacles on all the

The Wizard may be a very bad wizard, but he can still perform tricks – his green glasses have fooled people for many years.

people, so that everything they saw was green. I have been good to the people and they like me, but one of my greatest fears was the Witches of the East and West. You can imagine how pleased I was when I heard your house had fallen on the Wicked Witch of the East. I was willing to promise anything if you would do away with the other Witch. But, now that you have melted her, I am ashamed to say that I cannot keep my promises."

"I think you are a very bad man," said Dorothy.

"Oh, no, my dear, I'm really a very good man, but I'm a very bad Wizard."

"Can't you give me brains?" asked the Scarecrow.

They saw a little old man.

"You don't need them. But come to me tomorrow, and I will stuff your head with brains."

"How about my courage?" asked the Lion.

"You have plenty," answered Oz. "True courage is in facing danger when you are afraid. But if you come to me tomorrow I will see what I can do."

"How about my heart?" asked the Tin Woodman.

"I think you are wrong to want a heart. It makes most people unhappy. But you shall have a heart," said Oz, with a smile.

"How am I to get back to Kansas?" asked Dorothy.

"We shall have to think about that," replied the little man.

The next morning the Wizard took bran and filled the top of the Scarecrow's head. "You will be a great man," said the Wizard, "for I have given you bran-new brains."

Oz took a pretty heart made of silk and put the heart in the Woodman's breast. "There," said he, "now you have a heart that any man might be proud of."

The Wizard took a green bottle, the contents of which he poured into a dish.

"What is it?" asked the Lion.

"Courage," answered Oz. "But courage is always inside one, so this cannot be called courage until you have swallowed it."

The Lion drank.

Oz smiled and said to himself, "It was easy to make the Scarecrow and the Lion

The Scarecrow, the Tin Woodman, and the Lion already have the things they are looking for inside them. To help them believe this, the Wizard gives them each a keepsake.

and the Woodman happy, because they imagined that I could do anything. But it will take more than imagination to carry Dorothy back to Kansas, and I don't know how it can be done."

For three days Dorothy heard nothing from Oz. These were sad days for Dorothy, even though her friends were happy and contented.

On the fourth day Oz sent for her. "Well," said the little man. "It is quite beyond my powers to make a cyclone like the one that brought you here, but I believe I can make a balloon. If you will help me sew the silk together, we will begin work."

Dorothy's friends were happy.

So Dorothy took her needle and as fast as Oz cut the strips of silk, the girl sewed them neatly together.

When it was ready, Oz sent word to his people that he was going to visit a brother Wizard in the clouds and ordered the balloon to be carried out in front of the Palace.

Oz got into the basket and said to all the people, "While I am gone the Scarecrow will rule over you. I command you to obey him as you would me. Come, Dorothy! Hurry up, or the balloon will fly away."

At that moment, Toto ran into the crowd to bark at a kitten. Dorothy went after him, picked him up, and ran toward the balloon.

"I can't come back, my dear," called Oz. "Good-bye!"

She was within a few steps of it, when *crack!* went the ropes, and the balloon rose into the air without her.

"Come back," she screamed, "I want to go, too!"

"I can't come back, my dear," called Oz. "Good-bye!"

And that was the last any of them saw of Oz the Wonderful Wizard, though he may have reached Omaha safely, and be there now, for all we know. ❖

Away to the South

THE MORNING after the balloon went up, the Scarecrow sat on the big throne. "If Dorothy could be contented in Emerald City, we might all be happy together."

"But I want to go to Kansas and live with Aunt Em and Uncle Henry!" cried Dorothy.

The Scarecrow started to think. Finally, he said, "Why not call the Winged Monkeys, and ask them to carry you?"

"That's a good idea," said Dorothy joyfully. She spoke the magic words, and soon the Monkeys flew in through the open window and stood beside her.

"This is the second time you have called us," said the Monkey King. "What do you wish?"

"I want you to fly with me to Kansas," said Dorothy.

"We belong to this country alone, and cannot leave it," said the Monkey King, and with a bow, he flew away, followed by all his band. Dorothy was ready to cry. "I have wasted the charm to no purpose."

The Scarecrow was thinking again. "Let us call the soldier by the door and ask his advice."

So the soldier was summoned.

"Is there no one who can help me?" asked Dorothy earnestly.

Enchanted forests appear in many fairy tales. In Baum's forest, the magical trees use their branches like arms to stop unwanted travelers from passing through.

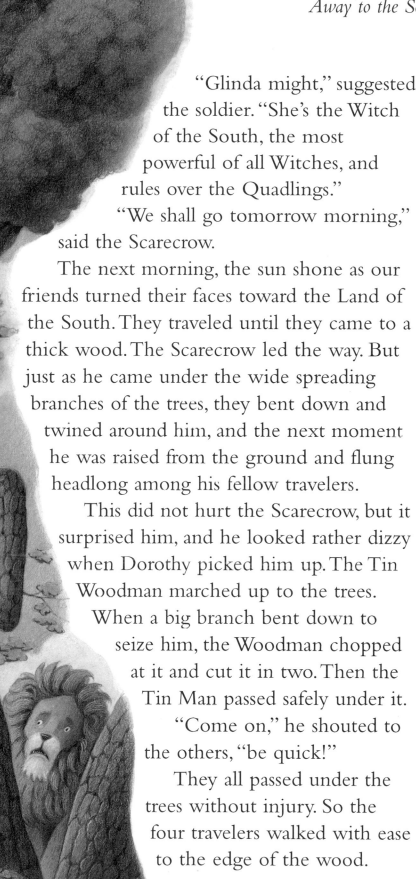

"Glinda might," suggested the soldier. "She's the Witch of the South, the most powerful of all Witches, and rules over the Quadlings."

"We shall go tomorrow morning," said the Scarecrow.

The next morning, the sun shone as our friends turned their faces toward the Land of the South. They traveled until they came to a thick wood. The Scarecrow led the way. But just as he came under the wide spreading branches of the trees, they bent down and twined around him, and the next moment he was raised from the ground and flung headlong among his fellow travelers.

This did not hurt the Scarecrow, but it surprised him, and he looked rather dizzy when Dorothy picked him up. The Tin Woodman marched up to the trees. When a big branch bent down to seize him, the Woodman chopped at it and cut it in two. Then the Tin Man passed safely under it.

"Come on," he shouted to the others, "be quick!"

They all passed under the trees without injury. So the four travelers walked with ease to the edge of the wood.

The branches of the trees twined around the Scarecrow.

To their surprise, they found a high
wall made of white china in front of them.
They climbed to the top of the wall and looked
down and saw houses made of china, the biggest of them
reaching only as high as Dorothy's waist. There were also
pretty little barns, and cows and sheep and horses, all made
of china.

Everything was made of china.

There were shepherdesses with bright-colored bodices,
princesses with gorgeous frocks, and shepherds dressed in
breeches with pink and blue stripes, princes with jeweled crowns,
and funny clowns – all made of china. The travelers began walking
through the country.

"We must be careful here," said the kind-hearted Woodman, "or
we may hurt these pretty little people."

A beautiful princess started to run away. Dorothy wanted to see
more of the Princess, and ran after her, but the china girl cried out,
"Don't chase me! I might fall and break myself. One is never so
pretty after being mended."

Indeed, a little clown came walking toward them, and Dorothy
could see that he was completely covered with cracks and had been
mended in many places.

They walked carefully. The little animals and all the people
scampered out of their way, fearing the strangers would break them.
After an hour or so, the travelers reached the other side of the
country and climbed the china wall.

The friends entered another forest and soon they came to an
opening where there were wild beasts of every kind. There were

tigers and elephants and bears and wolves and foxes.
For a moment Dorothy was afraid, but the Lion explained
that the animals were holding a meeting. As he spoke, the beasts
caught sight of him. The biggest tiger bowed, saying, "Welcome, O
King of Beasts! You have come in good time. We are threatened by
a tremendous monster – a great spider as big as an elephant."

"If I put an end to your enemy will you obey me as King of the
Forest?" inquired the Lion.

All the beasts roared, "We will!"

"Take good care of these friends of mine," said the Lion. And he
marched proudly away to do battle.

The great spider was lying asleep when the Lion found him. It
had a huge mouth, with a row of long, sharp teeth. The Lion gave a
great spring and landed on the monster's back. With one blow of his
heavy paw, armed with sharp claws, he knocked the
spider's head from its body.

When he knew it was quite dead, the
Lion went back to where the beasts were
waiting and said, "You need fear your
enemy no longer."

The beasts bowed down to the Lion as
their King, and he promised to come back
and rule over them as soon as Dorothy
was safely on her way to Kansas.

The Lion gave a great spring.

The four travelers passed through the rest of the forest in safety and soon saw a steep hill covered with great pieces of rock.

Suddenly, a head appeared and said, "This hill belongs to us, and we don't allow anyone to cross it."

Then from behind a rock stepped the strangest man the friends had ever seen. He was short and stout and had a big flat head supported by a neck full of wrinkles. But he had no arms at all.

The Scarecrow did not fear such a helpless creature. "I'm sorry, but we must pass over your hill," and he walked boldly forward. As quick as lightning the man's head shot forward and his neck stretched out until the top of his head struck the Scarecrow and sent him tumbling down the hill. A chorus of laughter came from the other rocks, and Dorothy saw hundreds of armless Hammer-Heads upon the hillside.

The Lion became angry and dashed up the hill.

Again a head shot swiftly out, and the Lion went rolling down the hill as if he had been struck by a cannon ball.

As Dorothy ran to help the Scarecrow, the Lion said, "It is useless to fight people with shooting heads."

"Call the Winged Monkeys," suggested the Tin Woodman.

The Lion went rolling down the hill.

"You have the right to command them once more." Dorothy uttered the magic words. The Monkeys were as prompt as ever. "What is your command?" asked the King of the Monkeys.

"Carry us over the hill," said Dorothy.

At once the Winged Monkeys caught the four travelers up in their arms. They carried Dorothy and her comrades to safety and set them down in the beautiful country of the Quadlings.

"This is the last time you can summon us," said the leader, "so good-bye and good luck."

The country of the Quadlings seemed rich and happy. The fences and houses were all painted bright red. The Quadlings were short and fat and were themselves dressed all in red.

They came to a beautiful castle.

After a while, the travelers came to a beautiful castle. Before the gates were three girls, dressed in red uniforms. As Dorothy approached, one of them asked, "Why have you come to the South Country?"

"To see the Good Witch," Dorothy answered.

The girl went into the castle. After a few moments, she came back to say that Dorothy and the others were to be admitted at once.

The friends were shown into a big room where the Witch Glinda sat upon a throne of rubies. She was very beautiful. Her eyes looked kindly upon Dorothy while she told her all about the wonderful adventures they had had.

Dorothy said one last good-bye.

"But my greatest wish is to get back to Kansas," said Dorothy.

Glinda kissed the sweet face. "I can tell you a way to get back to Kansas. But if I do, you must give me the Golden Cap."

"Willingly!" exclaimed Dorothy.

The Witch said to the Scarecrow, "What will you do when Dorothy has left us?"

"I will return to the Emerald City," he replied, "for Oz has made me its ruler."

"Then I shall command the Winged Monkeys to carry you to the Emerald City." Turning to the Tin Woodman, Glinda asked, "What will become of you?"

"The Winkies want me to rule over them," said the Tin Woodman.

Just as the Scarecrow, the Tin Woodman, and the Lion already had the things they looked for, so Dorothy always had the power to go home — if only she had known how to use it!

"My second command to the Winged Monkeys," said Glinda, "will be that they carry you safely to the land of the Winkies."

Then the Witch looked at the Lion. "What will become of you?"

"Over the hill of the Hammer-Heads," he answered, "lies a forest. The beasts there have made me their King."

"My third command to the Winged Monkeys," said Glinda, "shall be to carry you to your forest. Then, having used up all the powers of the Golden Cap, I shall give it to the King of the Monkeys, so that all the Winged Monkeys may be free at last."

"But you have not yet told me how to get back to Kansas," Dorothy exclaimed.

"The silver shoes can carry you to any place in the world. All you have to do is knock the heels together three times."

Dorothy was overjoyed. She threw her arms around the Lion's neck. Then she kissed the Tin Woodman and hugged the Scarecrow. She found she was crying at parting from her loving friends.

Glinda gave the girl a good-bye kiss, and Dorothy thanked her for all her kindness.

Dorothy took Toto in her arms, said one last good-bye, and clapped the heels of her shoes together three times, saying, "Take me home."

Aunt Em saw Dorothy.
"My darling child," she cried.

Instantly, she was whirling through the air. Then, she stopped suddenly and rolled over several times. When she sat up, she was sitting on the broad Kansas prairie. Toto jumped out of her arms, barking joyously.

Dorothy looked at her feet. She had lost the silver shoes in her flight.

Aunt Em had just come out of the house when she saw Dorothy. "My darling child," she cried, folding the little girl in her arms and covering her with kisses, "where in the world did you come from?"

"From the land of Oz," said Dorothy. "And oh, Aunt Em! I'm so glad to be home again!" ❖

From Kansas to Oz

DOROTHY'S ADVENTURES begin in Kansas, which lies in the center of the US. During the 19th century, many people moved into the Midwest, hoping to farm the treeless land. Gradually, this huge, flat area became home to a successful farming community.

While Dorothy comes from Kansas, the Wizard comes from Omaha in Nebraska.

Today, Kansas is a major wheat-growing area.

❖ A TOUGH LIFE

Life was not easy for the settlers – the harsh climate, risk of drought, and high winds, made day to day living a struggle. In the story, the word *gray* is used many times to describe life in Kansas. Dorothy has to rely on her dog Toto to keep her smiling! Luckily, colorful adventures are just around the corner ...

The Monkeys fly in

The Winkies

The Wicked Witch of the West's castle

THE WEST

Yellow is the color of the Winkies' land. Controlled by the cruel Witch of the West, this land has become stony and dry.

The land of Oz is surrounded by desert.

Oz is everything that Kansas isn't – colorful, varied, and full of adventures. But despite the grayness of Kansas, Dorothy wants to return there because it's her home. Here is the map of her journey through Oz.

Each land Dorothy visits is associated with a different color – her house falls in Munchkin land, where the people dress in blue.

The Sparkling Emerald City

THE NORTH

Friendly mice

A poppy field

A stork

A pack of wolves attack

The fierce Kalidahs

The enchanted wood

The Land of the China People

The Lion

The Tin Woodman

THE EAST

The Scarecrow

The deadly spider

The Munchkins

The Hammer-Heads

The Quadling people always dress in red. They are ruled by Glinda, the Witch of the South. Quad means four – so this is the fourth country in Oz.

THE SOUTH

Dorothy and Toto

Dorothy's house lands here and kills the Witch of the East

The Witch of the North

The Road to Oz

L. FRANK BAUM PUBLISHED *The Wonderful Wizard of Oz* in 1900. His modern American fairy tale was immediately loved by children throughout the US. Over the next few years, Baum wrote many more stories about Oz. But the popularity of his magical land had only just begun – Baum's characters were soon on the road to international fame.

W.W. Denslow's illustrations from the first edition of The Wizard of Oz.

❖ OZ ON STAGE

In 1902, Baum turned *The Wizard of Oz* into a musical. It was a big hit on Broadway in New York. There were many special effects, such as a snowstorm that woke Dorothy from her sleep in the poppy field.

❖ SILENT OZ

In 1925, several years after Baum's death, a silent film of *The Wizard of Oz* was made. The film changed Baum's story in various ways: Dorothy is eighteen, becomes Queen of Oz, and stays in Oz forever.

❖ A DREAM COME TRUE

The Wizard of Oz really took the world by storm in 1939, when it was made into a film musical, starring Judy Garland as Dorothy. The producers used Technicolor and special effects in a way they had never done before. Once again, Baum's story was changed – this time Dorothy's adventures were shown to be nothing but a dream!

The opening scenes were filmed in black and white to reflect the grayness of Kansas.

In the film, Dorothy's shoes are ruby, not silver, because the film-makers wanted to use strong colors.

❖ THE WONDERFUL WORLD OF OZ

The film was such a success that today few people think of Oz without remembering Judy Garland and her friends. But it was Baum's colorful imagination that made it all possible. He created a world where everyone, great or small, had what they searched for inside them — a place where dreams really could come true.

In the film, unlike the book, the Emerald City really is green — no glasses are needed!

In the film, the world of Oz is a dream world. The characters Dorothy meets are familiar faces from her life in Kansas.

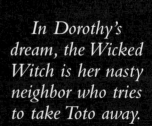

In Dorothy's dream, the Wicked Witch is her nasty neighbor who tries to take Toto away.

L. Frank Baum

*L. Frank Baum
(1856–1919)*

LYMAN FRANK BAUM was born in Chittenango, New York, in 1856. He tried a variety of careers, including reporter, window dresser, salesman, and theater manager, but nothing seemed to hold his attention for long. It was only when he decided to publish the stories he had been telling to his four sons that he made his name.

One of Baum's many careers was as a window dresser for a store.

Baum's friend, W.W. Denslow illustrated the first edition.

❖ SUCCESSFUL DAYS

At first, publishers were reluctant to accept a modern American fairy tale, but in 1900, the first edition of *The Wonderful Wizard of Oz* was published. Legend has it that Baum could not think what to call his imaginary land until he looked at his filing cabinet and saw A–N and O–Z. And so Oz was born.

❖ OZ FOREVER

In 1903, Baum moved to Hollywood, in California, with his family. He wrote many children's books, including thirteen more Oz books, in response to the success of *The Wizard of Oz.*